A Valentine for Tommy

by Wendy Wax

illustrated by Robert Roper

Ready-to-Read

Simon Spotlight/Nickelodeon

New York   London   Toronto   Sydney   Singapore

Based on the TV series *Rugrats*® created by Arlene Klasky, Gabor Csupo, and
Paul Germain as seen on Nickelodeon®

SIMON SPOTLIGHT
An imprint of Simon & Schuster Children's Publishing Division
1230 Avenue of the Americas
New York, New York 10020

Manufactured in the United States of America
First Edition
2 4 6 8 10 9 7 5 3 1

Library of Congress Cataloging-in-Publication Data

Wax, Wendy.
A valentine for Tommy / by Wendy Wax.
p. cm. — (Ready-to-read ; #12)
Based on the TV series Rugrats.
Summary: Tommy and the other babies create chaos in the department store
when they try to free his valentine hippo Harry from a window display.
ISBN 0-689-85256-8
[1. Hippopotamus—Fiction. 2. Toys—Fiction. 3. Department
stores—Fiction. 4. Valentine's Day—Fiction. 5. Babies—Fiction.]
I. Title. II. Series.
PZ7.W35117 Val 2003
[E]—dc21   2002006304

On Valentine's Day, Tommy
got a box from Grandpa Lou
and Lulu.

Inside was a hippo
named Harry.

Stu read the tag on Harry:

" 'I Need a Little Lovin'.' "

4

"A little oven!" Tommy said.

"Where are we going to get that?"

Didi called Betty.

"There is a Valentine's Day sale on pajamas," she said.

"We should take the babies shopping."

"Good idea," said Betty.

Tommy left Harry at home.

He waved good-bye

as they drove away.

When they got to the store,
Charlotte and Angelica were
on their way to buy pajamas too.
"Look who is here!" said Didi.

8

Tommy could not believe

his eyes.

Harry was in the store window,

staring right at him!

HARRY
THE HIPPO!

"How did *you* get

here, Harry?" Tommy asked.

"He cannot hear you,"

said Angelica. "He is

all locked-up."

"Maybe he escaped from home because he really needs to find that little oven," suggested Chuckie.

"We need to get him one afore someone takes him away!" exclaimed Tommy.

"Cute pajamas, right?"

Betty exclaimed.

Wheee!

The moving stairs took the babies to the second floor.

"I hope I win the jelly bean counting contest," said a girl on her way down.

"Wow!" said Tommy

when he saw the jelly beans.

"Whoever counts the most

wins," Angelica explained.

"I count one million

and six—I win!"

"One, two, free . . .
one, two, free,"
counted the babies,
popping jelly beans into
their mouths. "Yum!"

JELLY BEAN
COUNTING
CONTEST

I'M
UP

"We should get out of here!"

Chuckie said.

Then Tommy's eyes lit up.

"Come on, guys!

I know where to find

a little oven for Harry."

Kimi peered around
the giant dollhouse.
"How is this?" she asked,
holding up a tiny oven.
"Great!" said Tommy.
"Harry will love it!"

"Harry never told me his whole family lived here," Tommy said, gasping. "He probably got lost trying to find them."

I NEED A LITTL LOVIN'

HARRY

"They are all twins, Lil!"

said Phil.

"They look more alike

than we do," said Lil.

"We should bring Harry

a sister to play with,"

said Chuckie.

"Yeah, he is all alone

in the window,"

said Tommy sadly

as he reached for a hippo.

"Oops!"

"I guess they *all* want to visit Harry. He is almost as popular as me!" said Angelica.

"They sure must miss him," said Tommy.

"Those people do not look too happy," said Chuckie.

"Oops!" said Lil. "I think we cut in front of them."

"I had no idea they were in line for this ride with the moving stairs," said Phil.

PAJAMAS

"Look!" said Tommy.

"There is Harry."

The babies walked over to

the display-window entrance.

"Now we can bring him back home," said Kimi. "Maybe this is not such a good idea . . . ," said Chuckie.

"Hi, Harry," said Tommy.

"Here is your little oven.

And here is your sister

to keep you company."

"I love you,"

Tommy said, sniffling.

"But you should stay with

your family. You can come

visit me anytime you want."

"Look, Tommy, new pajamas
for you and Dil!"
exclaimed Didi.
"Do you like what I got
for you, pups?"
Betty asked Phil and Lil.

"Red is your color, princess.
These are perfect for you,"
Charlotte said to Angelica.
"I am glad I do not have to
wear those things,"
Kimi whispered to Chuckie.

"Harry!" Tommy said.

"You came back!

So you *do* love me

as much as I love you."

Tommy gave Harry a big hug. "Maybe your brothers and sisters can come play with us sometime," Tommy said.

"I am sorry you left your little oven at the store, Harry," Tommy said at bedtime. "We will get another one when we visit your family. Maybe we can get a little sink, too."